Before reading

Look at the book co[ver]
Ask, "What do you th[ink]

Turn to the **Key Word** [... wit]h
the child. Draw their
the tall letters and th[... readi]ng

During reading

Offer plenty of support and praise as the child reads the story. Listen carefully and respond to events in the text.

When a **Key Word** is used for the first time, it is also shown at the bottom of the page. If the child hesitates over a word, point to the **New Key Words** box and practise reading it together. If the word is phonically decodable, you can sound out the letters and blend the sounds to read the word ("d-o-g, dog"). Praise the child for their effort, then return to the story.

Pause every few pages and ask questions to check the child's understanding of what they have read. If they begin to lose concentration, stop reading and save the page for later.

Celebrate the child's achievement and come back to the story the next day.

After reading

After reading this book, ask, "Did you enjoy the story? What did you like about it?" Encourage the child to share their opinions.

Use the comprehension questions on page 54 to check the child's understanding and recall of the text.

Ladybird

Series Consultant: Professor David Waugh
With thanks to Kulwinder Maude

LADYBIRD BOOKS

UK | USA | Canada | Ireland | Australia
India | New Zealand | South Africa

Ladybird Books is part of the Penguin Random House group of companies
whose addresses can be found at global.penguinrandomhouse.com.
www.penguin.co.uk   www.puffin.co.uk   www.ladybird.co.uk

Penguin
Random House
UK

Original edition of Key Words with Peter and Jane first published by Ladybird Books Ltd 1964
Series updated 2023
This book first published 2023
001

With thanks to Liz Pemberton for her contributions in advising on the illustrations
With thanks to Inclusive Minds for connecting us with their Inclusion Ambassador network,
and in particular thanks to Guntaas Kaur Chugh for her input on the illustrations

Printed in China

The authorized representative in the EEA is Penguin Random House Ireland,
Morrison Chambers, 32 Nassau Street, Dublin D02 YH68

A CIP catalogue record for this book is available from the British Library

ISBN: 978-0-241-51085-8

All correspondence to:
Ladybird Books
Penguin Random House Children's
One Embassy Gardens, 8 Viaduct Gardens, London SW11 7BW

MIX
Paper from
responsible sources
FSC® C018179

Key Words

with Peter and Jane

5a

We like animals

Based on the original
Key Words with Peter and Jane
reading scheme and research by William Murray

Original edition written by William Murray
This edition written by Chitra Soundar
Illustrated by Flora Aranyi
Based on characters and design by Gustavo Mazali

an   animal   be

big   cat   do

grandad   granny

her   him   his

horse   let   little

my   not   off

pond   put   thank

there   thing   what

will   work

animal

big

cat

grandad

granny

horse

little

pond

Peter and Jane are helping mum.

"I will put the big things here," says Jane.

"And I will put the little things here," says Peter.

9

"What work will we do, Mum?" Jane says.

"We will work on this home for little animals," Mum says.

"Let me get the tool box," says Jane.

"Will you help me and Mum with this work, Peter?" Jane says.

He says he will help her, and Jane says thank you.

Peter picks up his tool. "What do we do with this?" says Peter.

"Hit that bit," says Jane.

"Look! The cat is there, Jane," Peter says. "He wants to help!"

"We are working," says Jane. "Hop off, little cat."

Dad has things to do at the shops. He lets Peter and Jane go with him.

Peter and Jane like doing things with Dad.

"There is the big bus!" says Peter.

Off they go.

New Key Words

him

17

On the bus, Jane says,
"We can sit there."

Peter sees a boy with
a little box.

"What is in there?"
Peter says to him.

"An animal," says the boy.

an

"Let's jump off here,"
Dad says.

Peter, Jane and Dad
get off at the shops.

"There is the big pet
shop," says Peter.

"Are there cats in that shop?" Peter says.

"No, they will not have an animal like that in there," Jane says.

"Let's go in here, Peter," says Dad.

23

"What will we get?"
says Peter.

"Let's get things to cook,"
says Dad.

He lets Peter get things
off the shelf.

"Thank you," says Dad.

"The big bus is here.
Off we go!" Jane says.

"What will we do at
home, Dad?" says Peter.

"We will cook things for
Granny and Grandad,"
Dad tells him.

New Key Words

granny   grandad

27

"Will you let me
work with you, Dad?"
says Peter.

"That will be a big help,"
Dad says. "Thank you,
Peter."

"I can do little things
to help," says Peter.

29

Peter says, "Will Granny and Grandad like my cooking?"

"Yes, they will," says Dad. "Tess seems to like it!"

"My cooking is not for an animal," Peter says. "Off you go, Tess."

Granny and Grandad
are here.

"Thank you for cooking,
Peter," says Granny. "Let's
go to the big pond. We will
see some animals there."

Peter and Jane will have a go on some horses.

"Can I go on his big horse, Jane?" asks Peter.

"Yes!" says Jane. "It will be fun for me to go on her little horse."

Have a go!

"Will you help me up on my big horse?" says Peter.

"There you are," the boy says. "Off you go."

Peter thanks him.

There goes Jane on her little horse.

Granny and Grandad are near the pond.

"Do not fall off, Jane!" they say to her.

Peter and Jane jump off the horses near the pond.

"What work is that girl doing there?" Jane asks Grandad.

"She is clearing weeds in the pond," says Grandad. "Her work will be a big help to the animals."

They go home. Mum and Dad are there!

"There are some animals at the big pond," says Peter.

"Granny and Grandad let me go on a little horse!" says Jane.

New Key Words

43

Jane is working on a gift for Granny and Grandad.

There is a little horse and a big pond in it.

Peter is with Granny and Ben the cat.

Peter puts the little cat on his red swing.

He jumps off.

"The cat will not sit," Peter says.

"Let him jump off, Peter," says Granny.

Jane gives Grandad
and Granny her gift.

"There is the pond,"
Granny says.

"There is the little horse,"
Grandad says.

"Good work, Jane.
Thank you," say Granny
and Grandad.

New Key Words

"Do you want to see
my gift for Granny and
Grandad?" Jane says
to her dad.

"I like the horse!"
says Dad.

"There is the pond," Peter
tells his dad. "A girl was
working near the pond."

New Key Words

"I want to work with horses," Jane says.

"I want to work in the mud at the pond!" says Peter. "Thank you for letting me go there, Granny and Grandad."

New Key Words

53

Questions

Answer these questions about
the story.

1 What are Mum and Jane working
   on at the start of the story?

2 How do Peter, Jane and Dad get to
   the shops?

3 Where do Peter and Jane go with
   Granny and Grandad?

4 What is Jane's gift for Granny
   and Grandad?